LAUNDRY
DAY
OVERLOAD

by **Dorothy H. Price** illustrated by **Shiane Salabie**

PICTURE WINDOW BOOKS
a capstone imprint

Published by Picture Window Books, an imprint of Capstone.
1710 Roe Crest Drive, North Mankato, Minnesota 56003
capstonepub.com

Library of Congress Cataloging-in-Publication Data
Names: Price, Dorothy H., author. | Salabie, Shiane, illustrator.
Title: Laundry day overload / by Dorothy H. Price : illustrated by Shiane Salabie.
Description: North Mankato, Minnesota : Picture Window Books, an imprint of Capstone, [2023] | Series: Jalen's big city life | Audience: Ages 5-7. | Audience: Grades K-1. | Summary: When J.C. helps his mom do the laundry, he adds too much detergent, causing suds to overflow. But thankfully, he knows who to ask for assistance.
Identifiers: LCCN 2021047081 (print) | LCCN 2021047082 (ebook) | ISBN 9781666335026 (hardcover) | ISBN 9781666334982 (paperback) | ISBN 9781666341973 (pdf) | ISBN 9781666341980 (kindle edition)
Subjects: LCSH: Laundry—Juvenile fiction. | Mothers and sons—Juvenile fiction. | Helping behavior—Juvenile fiction. | CYAC: Laundry—Fiction. | Mothers and sons—Fiction. | Helpfulness—Fiction. | LCGFT: Picture books.
Classification: LCC PZ7.1.P752828 Lau 2023 (print) | LCC PZ7.1.P752828 (ebook) | DDC [E]—dc23
LC record available at https://lccn.loc.gov/2021047081
LC ebook record available at https://lccn.loc.gov/2021047082

Editorial Credits
Editor: Alison Deering; Designer: Tracy Davies;
Production Specialist: Katy LaVigne

Design Elements
Shutterstock: Alexzel, Betelejze, cuppuccino, wormig

Printed and bound in the USA. 4882

TABLE OF CONTENTS

MEET J.C.

Hi! My name is Jalen Corey Pierce, but everyone calls me J.C. I am seven years old. I live with Mom, Dad, and my baby sister, Maya. Nana and Pop-Pop live in our apartment building too. So do my two best friends, Amir and Vicky.

My family and I used to live in a small town. Now I live in a city with big buildings and lots of people. Come along with me on all my new adventures!

Chapter 1

LAUNDRY DAY

"Can I help with laundry today?" J.C. asked Mom one Saturday morning.

J.C. and his family lived in an apartment building. They didn't have their own washer and dryer.

Instead, everyone used the building's laundry room.

"Sure," Mom replied. "We can add it to your chore list. Dad can stay with Maya. She needs a nap."

"Sounds like a plan," Dad replied. He put Maya in her crib.

"Now I have three chores," J.C. said. "Cleaning my room, dusting the bookshelves, and helping with laundry."

J.C. helped Mom carry the laundry down the hall. He pressed the button. Then they got onto the elevator.

In the laundry room, Mom sorted the clothes into piles.

"Put each pile into a different washer," she told J.C. "Each load gets one scoop of detergent."

"Got it!" J.C. replied.

Chapter 2

SUDS, SUDS, SUDS

J.C. picked up a pile of dirty clothes. He put them into the washer. Then he looked for another machine. But the rest were taken.

Mom was busy sorting laundry. J.C. didn't want to bother her.

He put the rest of the clothes into the same machine. Then he added extra detergent. That way everything would be extra clean.

J.C. closed the door. Mom came over and added the coins. Then she pressed a few buttons to start the wash.

They sat down to wait. A few minutes later, a mound of suds started coming out of the machine.

"Uh-oh," J.C. said.

"What's wrong?" asked Mom. She looked up to see suds spilling everywhere. "J.C., how much detergent did you add?"

"Four scoops," J.C. said.

Mom frowned. "That's way more than *one*, J.C."

"I put all the clothes in one machine. The rest were taken," J.C. explained. "I added extra soap to make sure *all* the clothes were clean."

"One scoop would have done the trick," Mom replied.

"I'm sorry," J.C. replied.

"We need to get this fixed, fast!" Mom told him. "We're not the only family who uses the laundry room."

"I think I know who can help!" J.C. said.

Chapter 3

HELP IS ON THE WAY!

J.C. rushed down the hall.

Mr. Jackson, the maintenance

man, was in his office.

"Can you please help us in

the laundry room? There are

suds everywhere!" J.C. exclaimed.

"Sure can, young man. Let's go!" said Mr. Jackson. He grabbed a machine with a long handle and wheels.

In the laundry room, suds were still piling up. Mom didn't look happy.

"Looks like someone used a few too many scoops of detergent, huh?" Mr. Jackson said.

"We're very sorry. It's J.C.'s
first laundry day," Mom
explained.

"Don't worry. This machine
will suck up the suds in no time,"
said Mr. Jackson.

"Can I help?" J.C. asked.

"Sure," Mr. Jackson replied.

J.C. and Mr. Jackson took turns using the machine. No one could use the laundry room until they were done.

J.C. felt bad. Not following directions was *not* a good idea.

Chapter 4

EXHAUSTED

Finally, Mom and J.C.

went back to their apartment.

They had loads of clean clothes.

But J.C.'s shoes were wet from

helping Mr. Jackson.

"Laundry day sure was long," Dad said.

"We had a little laundry overload," said Mom. "But it won't happen again, right, J.C.?"

J.C. nodded. "Now I know one scoop means *one* scoop," he said. "And that if something goes wrong in the building, we're not the only ones dealing with it."

"That's right," Dad said. "It's different now that we live in an apartment instead of a house."

"I'm just glad laundry day is done," J.C. said.

"Until next week," Mom said with a wink.

GLOSSARY

chore (CHOR)—a job that has to be done regularly; washing dishes and taking out the garbage are chores

detergent (dih-TUR-juhnt)—a powder or liquid that is used to clean clothes and dishes

maintenance (MEYN-tuh-nuhns)—care or upkeep of something, like an apartment building

mound (MOUND)—a hill or pile

sort (SAWRT)—to separate

suds (SUHDZ)—the foam on soapy water

MY LAUNDRY ROOM

All laundry rooms are different. Draw a picture of the laundry room where you live. Label everything, including the washing machine and the dryer, plus laundry supplies like detergent and laundry baskets. If you live in an apartment building, don't forget to add things like the cash machine and chairs.

LET'S TALK

1. Do you help with household chores? Are they inside jobs, like doing laundry, or outside jobs, like taking out the trash? Talk about your favorite and least favorite chores.

2. J.C. was excited to help with laundry day, but he didn't listen to directions. Have you ever offered to help someone, but made a few mistakes along the way? How did you make things right?

3. J.C. learns that living in an apartment is different than living in a house. What are some other ways that they might be different?

LET'S WRITE

1. Think about some ways you can help with new household jobs over the next week. Write a list of things you can do, and share it with your family.

2. What if Mr. Jackson hadn't been in the maintenance office when J.C. went looking for him? Think of another way J.C. could have helped clean up all the suds.

3. Think about a time someone helped you in a tough situation. Write a thank-you note to that person. Have a grown-up help you mail it or send it by email.

Dorothy H. Price loves writing stories for young readers, starting with her first picture book, *Nana's Favorite Things*. A 2019 winner of the We Need Diverse Books Mentorship Program, Dorothy is also an active member of the SCBWI Carolinas. She hopes all young readers know they can grow up to write stories too.

Shiane Salabie is a Jamaica-born illustrator based in the Philadelphia tristate area. When she moved to the United States, she discovered her first true love: the library. Shiane later realized that she wanted to bring stories to life and uses her art to do so.